Love You From F

A Keepsake Book for Children in Foster Care

MW01093104

WRITTEN BY
Jamie Sandefer

ILLUSTRATED BY
Pamela Goodman

Love You From Right Here: A Keepsake Book for Children in Foster Care

Published by Lucid Books in Houston, TX.
www.LucidBooks.net

ISBN 10: 163296029X
ISBN 13: 9781632960290
eISBN-10: 163296113X
eISBN-13: 9781632961136

Special Sales: Most Lucid Books titles are available in special quantity discounts. Custom imprinting or excerpting can also be done to fit special needs. Contact Lucid Books at info@lucidbooks.net.

Dedicated to my family and to all the children I will always love from right here.
-JS

For my Mom.
-PG

When you're over there...

I'll love you from right here.

When you're kind of sad...

I'll always be right here.

When you're feeling scared...

I'll sit with you right here.

When you're kind of mad...

I'll wait for you right here.

When you're feeling glad...

I'll laugh with you right here.

When you're kind of nervous...
I'll cheer for you right here.

When you're feeling brave...

I'll clap for you right here.

When you're kind of hurt...

I'll fix you up right here.

When you're feeling happy...

I'll play with you right here.

And if you're over there...

I'll still love you from right here.

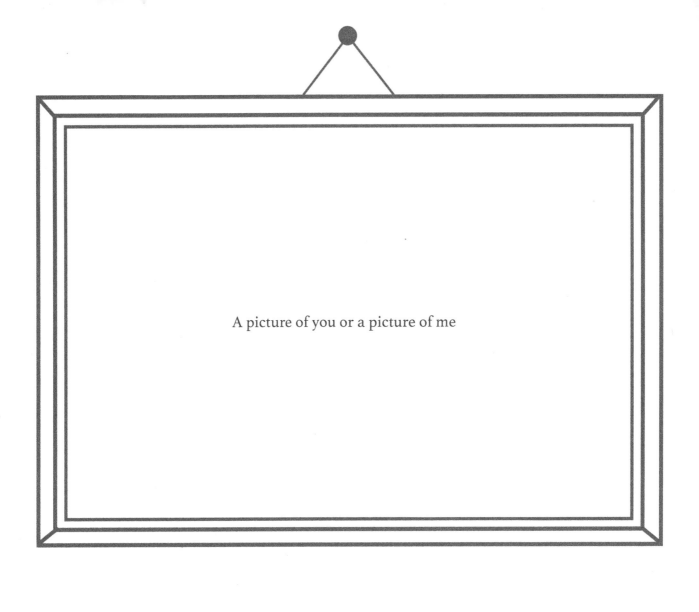

A picture of you or a picture of me

Arrival "Right Here" Date: _____

Departure "Over There" Date: _____

While You Were Right Here

The things you loved to eat:

_____

_____

_____

_____

The places you loved to go:

_____

_____

_____

_____

The things you loved to do:

_____

_____

_____

_____

The people you loved to see:

_____

_____

_____

_____

The things we love about you:

_____

_____

_____

_____

More about you...

_____

_____

_____

_____

_____

_____

_____

_____

_____

_____

About the Author and Illustrator

Jamie Sandefer is a stay-at-home mom and foster mom. She is passionate about advocating for children in foster care. In her spare time, she enjoys reading, being out-doors, and going to the beach. She and her family are avid Baylor Bears fans. Sic 'Em Bears! She resides in Texas with her husband and children.
Visit her at www.jamiesandefer.com

Pamela Goodman is a freelance illustrator in the San Francisco Bay Area and a graduate of the Academy of Art University. She illustrated "A Fish in Foreign Waters" and is working on writing and illustrating her own picture books. When not illustrating she loves to spend time digging in her garden or hiking with her husband and their dog Buko.
Visit her at www.pamelagoodman.com

CPSIA information can be obtained
at www.ICGtesting.com
Printed in the USA
BVHW020103071219
565718BV00009B/45/P